THIS WALKER BOOK BELONGS TO:

_____

_____

_____

_____

For Wendy Boase

First published individually as
Angel Mae, The Big Concrete Lorry (1989)
The Snow Lady (1990) and *Wheels* (1991)
by Walker Books Ltd, 87 Vauxhall Walk
London SE11 5HJ

This edition published 1998

2 4 6 8 10 9 7 5 3

© 1989, 1990, 1991 Shirley Hughes

This book has been typeset in Sabon.

Printed in Hong Kong

British Library Cataloguing in Publication Data
A catalogue record for this book is
available from the British Library.

ISBN 0-7445-6040-3

Tales of Trotter Street

Shirley Hughes

Angel Mae
— 7 —

The Big Concrete Lorry
— 21 —

Wheels
— 35 —

The Snow Lady
— 49 —

WALKER BOOKS
AND SUBSIDIARIES
LONDON · BOSTON · SYDNEY

Angel Mae

Mae Morgan lived with her mum and dad and her big brother Frankie in the flats on the corner of Trotter Street. Mae's grandma lived nearby. Soon there was going to be another person in the family, because Mae's mum was going to have a baby. It would be born around Christmas time.

Everyone was making preparations for the baby. Grandma was knitting little coats and booties. Dad was decorating the small bedroom. He painted the walls a beautiful yellow. Mum got out the old cradle that Mae and Frankie had slept in when they were babies. She put a pretty new lining in it.

"Imagine us being small enough to sleep in that!" said Frankie.

Mae tried sitting in the cradle. She could just fit if her knees were drawn up under her chin.

Mae thought about the baby a lot. She looked into her toy chest and pulled out some of her old toys. She was hoping to have some lovely new things at Christmas, so she thought she would give the baby a few of her old toys.

She didn't want to give away anything too special, like her best doll, Carol. She thought she could let the baby have her old pink rabbit and the duck who nodded his head and flapped his wings when you pulled him along. And there was the ball with the bell inside it. They were all too babyish for her now.

Carefully, Mae put the rabbit, the duck and the ball into the baby's cradle.

"What are you putting those old toys in there for?" asked Frankie. "Our new baby will be much too small to play with those." And he told Mae that at first it would be a tiny little baby, not nearly big enough to play with toys. "But he might like them when he's older," Frankie said.

"How do you know it will be a he?" Mae answered crossly.

Frankie said he didn't know, but he hoped it would be so he could teach the baby to play football.

Mae slowly piled up her old toys and threw them on the floor beside her toy chest.

The flat where Mae and Frankie lived was on the third floor. There were a good many stairs because there wasn't a lift. Mum got tired carrying up the shopping.

Mae got tired too. She wished she could be carried like a shopping bag.

"Carry me, carry me," she moaned, drooping on the banisters at the bottom step. But Mum couldn't carry Mae *and* the shopping. Mae was much too old to be carried anyway.

After lunch Mum sat down for a rest. Frankie put a cushion under her poor tired feet. Mae moped about. She counted Mum's toes – one, two, three, four – up to ten. Then she started to tickle her feet. But Mum didn't want her feet tickled just then. She lay back and closed her eyes but Mae knew she wasn't really asleep.

Mae went off to find Dad. He was getting ready to clean the car. He said that Mae could help if she liked, so together they went downstairs into the street. Dad gave Mae a rag so she could polish the hubcaps. Mae rubbed away until she could see her own face. It looked a bit funny.

"Do you think our baby will be a boy or a girl?" she asked.

"Nobody knows for sure," said Dad. "But as there's you and Mum and Grandma in our family already, it would even things up if it was a boy, wouldn't it?" He ruffled Mae's hair. "You'd like to have a baby brother, wouldn't you, Mae?"

But Mae said nothing. She just went on polishing.

At school, all the children were getting ready for Christmas. Mae's teacher, Mrs Foster, helped them to make paper robins and lanterns to decorate the classroom. Then Mrs Foster told everybody that they were going to act a play about baby Jesus being born. All the Trotter Street mums and dads would be invited to watch.

Nancy Jones was going to be Mary and wear a blue hood over her long fair hair and Jim Zolinski was going to be Joseph and wear a false beard. Frankie, Harvey and Billy were going to be kings. They had gold paper crowns with jewels painted round them.

Mae wanted to be a king too, but Mrs Foster said that kings were boys' parts. Mae looked into the wooden box which Mrs Foster had made into a manger for the baby Jesus. "I'll be baby Jesus, then," said Mae. She was sure she would fit into the manger if she tried very hard.

But Mrs Foster explained that they were going to wrap up a baby doll in a shawl to be baby Jesus. She said that Mae could be a cow or a sheep if she liked, but Mae certainly didn't want to be either of those. She stuck out her bottom lip and made a very cross face.

"What about being an angel?" asked Mrs Foster.

Mae didn't want to be an angel either.

"You could be the angel Gabriel," Mrs Foster told her. "That's a very special angel, a very important part."

Mae thought about this. Then she nodded her head.

"I'm going to be the angel Gave-you!" she told Frankie later.

"Angel who?" said Frankie.

"Angel Gave-you! A very special angel," said Mae proudly.

"I'm the angel Gave-you!" Mae announced, beaming, when Mum came to collect her. "Gave-you, Gave-you, Gave-you!" sang Mae as she bounced along ahead, all the way home.

"Angel Gave-you!" shouted Mae, hugging Dad round the waist when he came home from work.

"Gave me what?" asked Dad.

"Just Gave-you. That's my name in the Christmas play," Mae explained.

"Will you come and see us in it?" Frankie wanted to know.

Dad said he wasn't sure, but he would try very hard.

But when Mae and Frankie woke up on the morning of the Christmas
play, neither Mum nor Dad was there! Grandma was cooking breakfast.
She told them that Dad had taken Mum to the hospital in the night because
the new baby was going to be born very soon.

"Will they be back in time to watch me being the angel Gave-you?"
asked Mae anxiously.

"I'm afraid not," said Grandma. "But I'll be there for sure."

When Mae and Frankie arrived at school, the big hall looked very different. There was a blue curtain at one end with silver stars all over it and one big star hanging up in the middle. The smallest angels were going to stand on a row of chairs at the back. The animals were going to crouch down in front by the manger.

While the grown-ups were arriving, Mrs Foster helped the children to dress up. Mae had a white pillowcase over her front and a pair of white paper wings pinned on to the back. She was going to stand at the very end of the row because she was such a special angel.

From high up she could see all round the room. She could see all the mums and dads. Grandma was sitting in the very front row, smiling and smiling.

Then Mrs Foster sat down at the piano and all the children began to sing:

"Away in a manger, no crib for a bed,
The little Lord Jesus lay down his sweet head..."

Mary and Joseph sang, the angels sang and the animals sang. The shepherds came in and knelt down on one side of the manger. Then the three kings came in, carrying presents for baby Jesus. Mae sang very loudly.

15

Then she saw somebody coming in late at the very back of the room. It was Dad! He was smiling the biggest smile of all. Mae was so pleased to see him that she forgot she was in a play. She waved and shouted out, "Hello, Dad. I'm being the angel Gave-you!"

Dad put his fingers to his lips and waved back.

But Mae was waving so hard that her chair began to wobble ...

and Mae wobbled too ...

and then she fell right off the chair ...

She hit the floor with a horrible crash, wings and all!

Mrs Foster stopped playing the piano. All the children stopped singing. Everyone looked at Mae. Mae held her arm where it hurt. She stuck out her bottom lip. She wanted to cry. But she didn't. Instead, she climbed up on to the chair again and went on singing:

> *"The stars in the bright sky looked down where he lay,*
> *The little Lord Jesus asleep in the hay..."*

Then all the people in the audience smiled and clapped a special clap for Mae for being so brave and not spoiling the play. Grandma clapped harder than anyone.

"Good old angel Gave-you!" said Dad when it was all over.

Grandma gave Frankie and Mae a hug and said it was the best Christmas play she had ever seen.

Then Dad said he had a big surprise for them. They had a new baby sister, born that morning. And Mum was going to bring her home in time for Christmas!

When Mae and Frankie went to the hospital, they looked into the cot and saw their tiny baby sister wrapped up in a white shawl. She had a funny little, crumpled up, red face and a few spikes of hair standing on end, and tiny crumpled up fingers. Mae liked the way she looked and she liked her nice baby smell. She was pleased that the baby looked so funny.

18

But most of all she was pleased that Mum
would be home in time for Christmas.

The Big Concrete Lorry

The Patterson family lived at number twenty-six Trotter Street. There was Mum, Dad, Josie, Harvey and little Pete. Also Murdoch, their dog.

Their house had a patch of garden at the back with a flower-bed, a washing line and an apple tree. In front there was only just room between the house and the street for some flower-pots and a couple of dustbins.

Josie had a room of her own. It was jam-packed with *her* things.

Harvey and little Pete shared the back bedroom. It was jam-packed with *their* things.

Murdoch had a basket in the kitchen. But often (though he wasn't supposed to) he slept at the bottom of Harvey's bed. Murdoch was a roly-poly dog who fitted nicely under Harvey's feet, like a plump hot-water bottle.

The Pattersons' hall was full of coats, boots, skate-boards and buggies. The family living room was very often full of Pattersons. Sometimes – when Josie was doing her homework at one end of the table and Mum was cutting out a blouse at the other end, and Dad was eating his supper in front of the television, and little Pete was playing with his toy cars, and Harvey and Murdoch were flopping about all over the sofa – it seemed as though the room was so full it would burst!

"We must have more space!" moaned Mum.

"We could move to a bigger house," said Dad, "if only big houses weren't so expensive."

All the family said that they couldn't possibly move to a new house. They loved Trotter Street far too much.

Then Dad had a good idea. "We could build an extension!" he cried.

Harvey wanted to know what an extension was. Dad explained that it was an extra room at the back, just like the one which Mr Lal had built next door. Mr Lal's extension was full of beautiful pot-plants and ornaments.

All the Pattersons thought that to have an extension like Mr Lal's would be a very good idea. So Dad brought home some brochures showing pictures of splendid extensions with happy people looking out of them.

"I'll put it up myself!" said Dad.

"Are you sure you can manage it?" Mum asked anxiously.

Dad said that Mr Lal and his son Rhajit, and Frankie and Mae's dad from up the street, had promised to help him, so it would be all right.

23

Next week, a delivery van drew up outside the Pattersons' house and some men unloaded bits of wood and windows and doors and stacked them in the back garden. This was the extension, all in pieces.

"Now we need some bricks," said Dad.

A few days later another truck arrived. It had "JIFFY BUILDING CO" written on it and, underneath, "Joe and Jimmy Best".

"Load of bricks you ordered!" said jolly Joe Best, jumping down from the cab.

Then he and Jimmy lowered the flap at the back of the truck and began unloading the bricks. They took them through the house and stacked them in the garden.

After they had driven off, Harvey, Josie and little Pete had a great time playing on the bricks, while Mum vacuumed away the dirty footprints left by Joe and Jimmy.

The following morning, Dad got up very early and put on his old trousers, saying that he was going to dig a foundation. Of course, Harvey wanted to know what a foundation was. Dad explained that it was a solid base for the extension walls to stand on.

Mr Lal came round after breakfast and helped Dad measure the space for the extension. They marked it out carefully with string, pegged to the ground. Then Dad, Mr Lal and Rhajit, and Frankie and Mae's dad began to dig a trench following the line of the string.

Little Pete thought all this was very interesting. He fetched his spade and began to dig too. So did Murdoch.

26

When the trench was finished, the men cleared the space where the floor was to be, put down bits of brick and rubble and covered them with a plastic sheet. Now everything was ready for the concrete. But first, an Inspector came to look at it, to make sure it had all been done properly.

Meanwhile, Josie and Harvey pretended that the extension was already built and they were having lunch inside. Josie imagined that it had pink wallpaper and Harvey imagined that there were curtains with a pattern of aeroplanes.

Dad was so tired the next day that he didn't get up early. Mum took him a cup of tea in bed. While the rest of the family were having breakfast, they heard a great noise in the street.

They all hurried outside.
A lorry had arrived at their house. It was huge!
It had a big drum that turned slowly round and
round – CRRURK, CRRURK, CRRURK!
On the side of the lorry was written
"JIFFY READY-MIX
CONCRETE CO".

Out jumped jolly Joe Best. "Load of concrete you ordered!" he called cheerfully.

"Not this morning, surely?" said Mum. "I'm sure we didn't…"

But it was too late. Jimmy had already pulled a lever and the big drum poured out a load of concrete, all in a rush. Slop! Slurp! Dollop! Splosh! Just like that! It landed in a shivering heap right outside the Pattersons' front door.

Dad rushed downstairs, pulling on his trousers over his pyjamas. "We weren't expecting you today!" he shouted.

"That's OK. Just sign here," said Joe. Then he leapt back into his seat. "It's quick-setting!" he called from the cab window. "Be hard as a rock in a couple of hours. Better get busy!"

"But we haven't…" Dad called back.

But Jimmy was already revving up the engine. The big concrete lorry roared away up the street in a cloud of dust.

"Quick!" cried Dad, picking up a shovel.
"Quick!" shrieked Mum, searching for a spade.
"Grab those buckets!"
"Fetch the wheelbarrow!"
"Run for the neighbours!"
"The quick-setting concrete is soon going to set!"

Never had the Pattersons moved so fast.
Mum began to shovel up the concrete into the wheelbarrow and trundle it through the house, while Dad shovelled and smoothed it down over the foundation at the back.

Josie and Harvey ran to fetch Mr Lal and Rhajit from next door, and Frankie and Mae's dad from up the street.
And they all came running.

The neighbours pitched in and shovelled and spread too. Josie, Harvey and little Pete ran up and down with buckets. Murdoch joined in, barking loudly.

Everyone laboured and struggled and fell over one another's feet. They shovelled and heaved and trundled concrete from the front of the house to the back. And steadily the heap on the pavement grew smaller and smaller.

"Quick! It's beginning to set!" shouted Mum.

Everyone worked faster and faster.

"Done at last!" gasped Dad, throwing down his shovel and wiping his hands on his trousers.

Then all the workers rested. The foundation was finished. Only a small hill of concrete was left beside the front door. It had set so hard that nothing in the world would shift it.

The extension went up bit by bit. First, a low brick wall, then the roof, windows and door.

And at last the Patterson family were able to move in.

They were so pleased with their beautiful new extension that they gave a party for all their neighbours.

Harvey and little Pete were extra pleased with the small concrete hill which stood outside their front door. None of their friends had one like it. It was great for sitting on and for racing toy cars down.

And if you climbed up and stood on the top, you could see right to the very end of Trotter Street!

Wheels

Spring at last! The Easter holidays had arrived and the wheels were out on Trotter Street. Sanjit Lal zipped along on his roller-skates, wearing a smart crash-helmet. Little Pete Patterson rode his red tricycle, ring-a-ding-dinging the bell to let everyone know he was coming.

Harvey and Barney took turns on Barney's skate-board and Mae pushed her baby sister Holly in a brand new buggy. Some of the big girls and boys had wonderful, new full-size bikes, even racers! They gathered at the corner to show them off. Carlos and Billy had their old bikes.

Billy's mum looked after Carlos in the school holidays, while *his* mum was at work. When she took Billy's baby brother to the park in the afternoon, Carlos and Billy came too and brought their bikes. They were not old enough to ride on the road, of course. It was too dangerous.

The park was the best place to ride. There was a smooth, wide path which went round the play area then into a steep slope. You could whizz down it, cornering at high speed, and free-wheel the rest of the way, past the old band-stand until, braking gently, you ended up at the bottom by the lake where the ducks swam.

The little kids playing and the mums chatting on the benches and the old lady who came to feed the birds all stopped what they were doing and stared as Carlos and Billy flew past.

Whooosh!

There was a narrow, humpbacked bridge over the lake. Carlos and Billy thought it was exciting to race their bikes up one side and down the other. Sometimes Carlos won and sometimes Billy. But if Mr Low, the park-keeper, saw them, he soon put a stop to it. He was very strict about people behaving well in his park. Mr Low did not seem to like fast riding at all, not even on the paths.

Orville, his assistant, was not quite so strict. Sometimes, when Mr Low went off to have a cup of tea in his hut, Orville would call out encouraging things to Carlos and Billy as they raced by.

All the same, Carlos and Billy both wished they had better bikes.

"You can get up a lot more speed on a big bike," said Billy. "They have gears too."

"I've seen one I like in a shop," said Carlos. "Blue and silver with a pump to match."

"I'm going to ask for a new bike for my birthday," said Billy. "It's very soon now."

"It's my birthday soon as well," said Carlos, "and I'm going to get a new bike too."

Carlos asked his mum about this. He had asked her before and he asked her again that evening. But his mum said that new bikes were very expensive. She explained that it was difficult for her to save up for things like bikes. She worked in a bakery and often brought home nice fruit cake and cream buns for Carlos and his big brother Marco – but not very much money.

"Marco's got a proper bike," moaned Carlos.

"He's older than you," said Mum, "and he needs it for his Saturday job. He's saving up for a new mountain-bike. When you're bigger, you can learn to ride his old one."

"But I need a new bike *now*," Carlos said.

Mum only answered: "We'll have to see…"

On the afternoon of his birthday, Billy proudly brought his brand new bike to the park. It was orange, with shiny silver handlebars. Everyone gathered round to admire it. Even Orville left his work to come and have a look.

"Race you!" Billy called out to Carlos, as he pulled away and glided off down the path.

It was not much of a race. Billy won easily. Carlos felt silly pedalling furiously behind, crouched over the handlebars of his old bike. His legs felt too long and his knees kept getting in the way.

After a while Billy's mum suggested that Billy should give Carlos a turn on his new bike, which he very kindly did. But when Carlos had swooped down the hill like a bird once or twice, he had to give the beautiful bike back to Billy.

40

In the end, Carlos gave up wanting to race. There was no point. He threw down his old bike by the lake and sat by himself, tossing pebbles into the water.

He felt cross with Billy. He even felt cross with the ducks who came swimming over to see if he had any bread.

"You wait! You wait till it's my birthday!" he told them.

On the evening before his birthday, Carlos kept wondering if Mum had managed to get him a bike. He thought she could have hidden one in the shed behind their block of flats.

He even secretly slipped out and tried the shed door, but it was locked. Was there a bike inside? He looked through a crack, but he couldn't see anything. Mum had promised that tomorrow she would bring home a very special cake from the shop – a birthday cake for Carlos! She said that he could ask Billy round for tea. But Carlos didn't want Billy to come to his birthday tea.

In bed that night, Carlos was too excited to sleep.

He kept imagining getting a new bike: a big bike, a blue and silver bike, a bike that was even better and faster than Billy's, which he could show off in the park. He crept to the window and looked down at the shed. There was a light on in there! He could see it shining up through the skylight in the roof. He watched for a long time. Then he went back to bed.

In the morning, Mum gave Carlos a big birthday hug. Marco had gone off early, but he had left a card on the kitchen table with some bears in a spaceship and "Happy Birthday, Carlos" written inside it. There were some parcels on the table too, all wrapped in fancy paper.

"Aren't you going to open them?" asked Mum, beaming.

Carlos pulled off the papers one by one. There was a jigsaw puzzle, a new jacket in dazzling red and green, just like the ones the big boy bikers wore, and a toy car with remote control. Carlos had wanted one ever since he had seen them in a shop and he was very pleased. But he knew at once that there was no new bike.

"Marco's going to give you his present when he comes in at teatime," Mum told him.

Carlos knew that Marco's present could not possibly be a new bike. He would not have nearly enough money for that. Inside, Carlos could not help feeling bitterly disappointed.

When Mum asked him if he would like to go and play with Billy that morning and show him his new things, Carlos said no – he would rather go to the shop with Mum. So he took his new car and played with it in the back of the bakery while his mum served the customers. The car went very well. Everyone made a great fuss of Carlos when they heard it was his birthday. One lady bought him a chocolate cream cake and another gave him some money for his piggy-bank.

When they got home, Mum opened a box and brought out a truly wonderful cake. It was pink and white and covered in icing shells and swirls, with silver holders for the candles. There was a plate of fancy pastries too, and ice-cream. Carlos ate a lot of everything. But when the time came to light his candles, he missed having Billy to help him blow them out.

Then Marco walked in. He got hold of Carlos and swung him round, singing "Happy Birthday to you!" Then he ate a very large slice of cake.

"Want to find out what I've got for you?" said Marco. "Follow me."

Carlos followed Marco downstairs.
All the way down, Carlos was wondering
what Marco was going to give him.

He knew it could not be a bike.
So what was it? They walked right past
the shed. Then at last Carlos saw
his present!

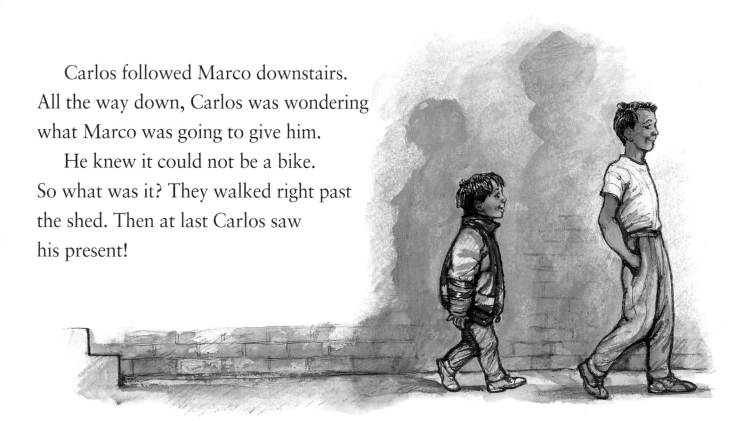

It was a go-cart! A real go-cart! It had proper steering and rubber wheels
and a seat, and it was painted bright red. Marco had made it himself. Carlos
was too surprised to speak. Never, ever, in his wildest dreams had he imagined
owning a go-cart! He looked at it for a long time. He stroked its wheels and its
little seat. Then he put his head against Marco's arm. "Thanks, Marco," he said.

It was the last day of the holidays. Most of Trotter Street had turned up in the park for the big event: the Non-Bicycle Race! The starters were already lined up – Sanjit, Sam and Ruby Roberts were on roller-skates; Harvey and Barney had skate-boards.

Jim Zolinski and Brains Barrington were in their box-on-wheels; Frankie had borrowed a scooter, and Mae and Debbie had one roller-skate each. Carlos was at the controls of his new go-cart, with Billy crouching behind him. Now Josie lifted the starter's flag…

Ready, steady, GO! Cheering mums, dads and toddlers lined the track. The Bird Lady was there and Orville too. Even Mr Low popped his head round the door of his hut to watch, though mostly to keep an eye on his flower-beds.

Past the play area, into the steep slope, gaining speed then cornering wildly, sometimes crashing but managing to scramble on again, weaving, coasting, trundling they went – all the way down to the lake.

And who came first?

Carlos and Billy in the wonderful go-cart,

of course!

The Snow Lady

Sam's real name was Samantha but everyone called her Sam. Sam's dog was named Micawber but everyone called him Mick. Sam and Mick were very fond of each other.

In the mornings, when Sam went to school and Sam's mum and dad and her big sister Liz went to work, Mick stayed at home to guard the house.

When school was over Sam walked home with her friend Barney and his dad. As soon as Mick heard Sam's footsteps he put his front paws on the window-sill and barked a joyful welcome. Sam longed to put him on his lead right away and run off up Trotter Street, with Mick pulling her along and sniffing excitedly at gates and lamp posts. But Mum was still at work and, as usual, she had arranged for Mrs Dean next door to keep an eye on Sam until everyone else came home.

49

Mrs Dean lived alone with her cat Fluff. Her house was very clean and tidy. The lace curtains were snowy white and the floor was polished like a skating rink. Mrs Dean welcomed Sam with a glass of milk and two plain biscuits. Sam balanced them on her lap and tried not to drop crumbs while she and Fluff and Mrs Dean sat side by side on Mrs Dean's beautiful blue sofa and watched television.

Mick was never allowed into Mrs Dean's house. He and Fluff got on very badly whenever they met. Sam could hear him howling mournfully next door.

"Whatever has got into that dog?" said Mrs Dean.

She opened her front door and shushed at Mick from the doorstep, but he didn't take a bit of notice. He just went on howling.

Sam and Mick were both glad when they heard Mum's key in the lock.

Mrs Dean's garden was just as neat and tidy as her house. If Mick got in there and started to dig holes searching for imaginary rabbits, or picked a fight with Fluff, Mrs Dean became very cross.

Mrs Dean didn't even like Mick to be in the street. Sam and Barney and the other children often played in Trotter Street after school and Mick always joined in. But before long Mrs Dean's face would appear at her window. She would tap sharply on the pane, then put out her head and say to Sam: "That dog really ought to be chained up. My poor little Fluff is so frightened she daren't come out." Or she would say: "Would you mind asking your friends not to sit on my wall?" Or: "A little less noise, dear, please."

And that was the end of their game.

51

But now the weather was getting too cold to play out of doors. One
night the water from a leaking drain froze on the pavement outside Sam's
house, turning it into a sheet of ice. The Trotter Street children had a great
time running up to it as fast as possible and seeing how far they could slide.
They hung on to one another and all slid together in a chain. Wheee! It was
just like the Winter Olympics! Mick ran alongside, skidding and barking.

Soon Mrs Dean popped out wearing a shawl over her shoulders.
"That's very dangerous," she said. "You might easily break your arms
or legs! Do stop at once."

Everyone stopped sliding except Barney. He was at the end
of the chain and just kept going. He cannoned into Harvey.
Harvey cannoned into Billy, who fell against Mae, who
slipped over, pulling Sam and the others with her.
There was a terrific pile-up.

"I'm glad Mrs Dean doesn't live next door to us," Barney said later, when he and Sam were drying their feet. "She's always interfering and she hardly ever smiles. She's an old meanie. Mean Mrs Dean, I call her!"

It was getting near to Christmas. People in Trotter Street were buying Christmas trees and putting up decorations. Mrs Dean hung a wreath of plastic holly tied with red ribbons on her door.

Everyone admired it except Mick, who took a savage dislike to it. He barked fiercely every time he caught sight of it. Sam had a terrible time trying to drag him past Mrs Dean's house whenever they went for a walk.

One day Mick got out on his own and worried the ribbon until he got one end of it between his teeth.

Then he pulled the whole thing down and ran off up Trotter Street with the wreath round his neck and the ribbons streaming out behind. Mrs Dean was very cross indeed. After that, Mick was in bad disgrace.

Sam was pleased when she heard Mrs Dean telling Mum that she was planning to spend Christmas with her married son. And sure enough, on the very day before Christmas Eve, Sam saw her setting out in a taxi, taking Fluff in a cat basket and a great many parcels. Hurrah! thought Sam.

Then something even better happened. Out of a slate-grey sky it began to snow. Big flakes whirled down, covering the pavements and parked cars of Trotter Street with a soft, white blanket.

Next morning the sun came out and so did Sam and Barney. They decided to build a snowman where the snow lay thickest, between Sam's front gate and Mrs Dean's. First they piled the snow into a big heap. Mick watched with interest.

Soon there was something which looked like a person with a round head, stick arms and stones for eyes, nose and mouth.

"Let's give him a top hat and a scarf and a pipe," said Barney. "Then he'll be a real snowman!"

Sam and Barney went indoors. Mum was busy but she said they could pick out some old clothes from the top of the cupboard if they liked.

But Sam and Barney could not find any of the things they wanted, only a lot of hats and dresses belonging to Mum and Liz.

"It'll just have to be a snow lady," Sam decided.

They dressed the snow lady in a hat and coat, put a shawl over her shoulders and hung a handbag on one of her stick arms. She looked very realistic.

"I know who she reminds me of," said Barney. And he moved the stones so that her mouth turned down instead of up.

He searched in the snow for some more small stones and arranged them where the snow lady's feet would have been. The words stood out clearly:

Sam giggled. The snow lady really did look rather like Mrs Dean. But Barney had not finished. He rearranged the D in Dean to make an M. Then the stones read:

"Lucky she's away," said Sam. "How awful it would be if she could see it!" Then they heard Mum calling and ran indoors taking Mick with them.

The rest of the day was so busy and exciting that Sam and Barney forgot all about the snow lady.

Late that night, long after Barney had wished them all a Happy Christmas and gone home to hang up his stocking, Sam was too excited to sleep. She got up, drew the curtains back a little and looked out at the street. Everything looked white and Christmassy, but big black clouds were scudding across the moon. When she caught sight of the snow lady, still standing there all alone, it gave her quite a shock.

Then Sam saw a taxi draw up. Out stepped Mrs Dean! The driver unloaded Fluff and the luggage and helped her into the house. Mrs Dean walked right past the snow lady without even glancing at her.

But she'll see her tomorrow when it's light, thought Sam. It will hurt her feelings. And on Christmas Day too!

Sam decided she must go out at once and kick away the stones which spelled out the snow lady's name. She would take off the clothes too. It was *terribly important!*

Sam crept quietly downstairs and began to put on her coat over her pyjamas. But Mick heard her and came running, barking and making a great fuss.

Mum put her head round the living room door. "Whatever are you doing, Sam? You can't go out at this time of night!" And she packed Sam firmly off upstairs. "The sooner you're asleep the sooner Christmas will be here," she said, kissing her good-night.

Still Sam could not get to sleep. She felt too awful about Mrs Dean. When she did fall asleep her dreams were full of excited visions of Mick, Fluff and the snow lady and lots of Christmas parcels all tied up with yards and yards of red ribbon. Mrs Dean was inside one of the parcels. She jumped out and then they were all running and running… But it was not feet which Sam heard in her sleep. It was rain.

When Sam woke
up it was still dark.
Christmas morning!
And yes, the stocking at
the foot of her bed was
full of exciting surprises.
But Sam did not put
on her light yet.

Instead she ran to
the window. She could hardly see out because rivulets of water were streaming
down the pane. Below, in the street, Sam could just see the snow lady. She
seemed to have slumped back against the gate post and all around her lay a
puddle of water.

Then a great, warm hope leapt up inside Sam. She skipped back into bed
and began to open her stocking.

As soon as Christmas Day had begun properly and all the family
had kissed each other and given their presents, Sam slipped
out of the front door.

It had stopped raining. The snow lady had
collapsed altogether. Her hat had fallen over
her face and her clothes were limp and dripping.

She kicked the stones and scattered them
about. Then she picked up the snow
lady's clothes and pushed
them into the dustbin.

She was only just in time. Mrs Dean's front door opened and out came Mrs Dean, dressed for church.

Mum hurried to their doorstep to call out "Merry Christmas, Mrs Dean! I didn't know you'd come back!"

"A merry Christmas to you all, Mrs Robinson. My son and his wife have flu and couldn't have me to stay after all," said Mrs Dean.

"Then of course you must come and have Christmas dinner with us," Mum said at once.

"Why, thank you! That's very kind," said Mrs Dean. And her face melted.

Sam stood right in front of what was left of the snow lady.
The name which had stood out so clearly in the snow was now just
a jumble of stones lying in a pool of water. Sam shuffled them about
with her feet, just in case.

"I expect you wish the snow had lasted longer," Mrs Dean
said to Sam.

"Oh no, I don't mind a bit, really," said Sam. And she gave Mrs
Dean one of her biggest most Christmassy smiles.

MORE WALKER PAPERBACKS
For You to Enjoy

Also by Shirley Hughes

THE NURSERY COLLECTION

Colours, shapes and sizes, sounds, opposites and numbers – these are the
concepts introduced to young children in this delightful nursery picture book,
which features a lively toddler and her equally engaging baby brother.

"Predictably first class… Concepts are introduced with domestic examples
and Hughes' characteristic gentle humour." *The Guardian*

0-7445-4378-9   £6.99

LET'S JOIN IN

Each of the books in this series for pre-school children takes a single
everyday verb and shows entertainingly some of its many meanings and applications.

"There's so much to look at, so much to read in these books."
Children's Books of the Year

0-7445-3652-9	BOUNCING
0-7445-3654-5	CHATTING
0-7445-3653-7	GIVING
0-7445-3655-3	HIDING

£4.50 each

OUT AND ABOUT

Eighteen richly illustrated poems portray the weather and
activities associated with the various seasons.

"Hughes at her best. Simple, evocative rhymes conjure up images that then
explode in the magnificent richness of her paintings." *The Guardian*

0-7445-6062-4   £6.99